THE WOODEN DRAGON

JOAN AIKEN

ILLUSTRATED BY BEE WILLEY

RED FOX

For David Donisthorpe Armstrong 1931-1999
who carved the dragon J.A.

For Ian Craig, with thanks B.W.

THE WOODEN DRAGON
A RED FOX BOOK 0 099 43958 1

First published in Great Britain by Jonathan Cape,
an imprint of Random House Children's Books

Jonathan Cape edition published 2004
Red Fox edition published 2005

1 3 5 7 9 10 8 6 4 2

Text copyright © Joan Aiken Enterprises Ltd, 2004
Illustrations copyright © Bee Willey, 2004

The right of Joan Aiken and Bee Willey to be identified as the author
and illustrator of this work has been asserted in accordance with
the Copyright, Designs and Patents Act 1988.

All rights reserved.

Red Fox Books are published by Random House Children's Books,
61–63 Uxbridge Road, London W5 5SA,
a division of The Random House Group Ltd,
in Australia by Random House Australia (Pty) Ltd,
20 Alfred Street, Milsons Point, Sydney, NSW 2061, Australia,
in New Zealand by Random House New Zealand Ltd,
18 Poland Road, Glenfield, Auckland 10, New Zealand,
and in South Africa by Random House (Pty) Ltd,
Endulini, 5A Jubilee Road, Parktown 2193, South Africa

THE RANDOM HOUSE GROUP Limited Reg. No. 954009
www.kidsatrandomhouse.co.uk
A CIP catalogue record for this book is available from the British Library.

Printed in Singapore

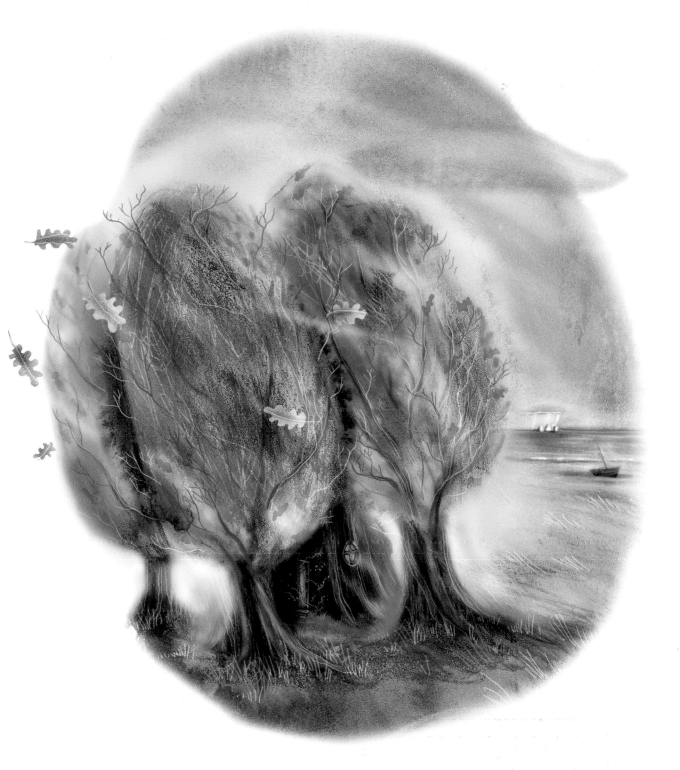

A brother and sister lived in a small house in a hollow.
He was called Handle. She was called Window.
A ring of big trees grew all round the house. In spring and
summer their leaves were green and made a cool shade from
the hot sun.

In autumn the leaves turned red. They fell off the trees. They lay so thick on the ground that the little house was buried right up to its bedroom windows. Each year Handle swept up all the leaves and burned them in a great bonfire. As he swept he sang a song he had made up about a friendly dragon.

'I wish you could help me with the sweeping,' Handle sometimes said to his sister.

But Window couldn't help him because she was lame. When she was small she had slipped on some fallen leaves and broken her leg. She could only walk very slowly.

'I wish I could help, too,' she said to Handle. 'But I can tell you stories while you do the sweeping.'

Window told wonderful stories, sitting in the sun outside the cottage door. People who were sick or sad or worried came to listen and often they were cured of their sickness or their sadness or their worry.

Handle was a sailor. Every few months he went off on his ship, sailing a long way over the sea. Sometimes he was gone for weeks and weeks. Window missed him very much when he was away. But she kept busy, knitting socks and jackets and woolly hats and scarves and gloves.

When her brother was away she stopped telling stories. People no longer came to hear them.

One day Handle said, 'Now I have to go on an extra long trip.'
'Oh dear,' said Window. 'Must you go?'
'Yes, I must,' he said. 'Sailors have to sail. But I have
made something to keep you company while I am gone.'

Handle was very clever at carving things from wood.
He had made his sister a little wooden dragon, no bigger
than a teapot, with one wing folded and one wing spread,
with two shining eyes and a pointed head, with a
hopeful mouth that looked as if it was ready to smile.

But Window hardly looked at the dragon. She was so
worried about Handle going away for so long. And about
the leaves.

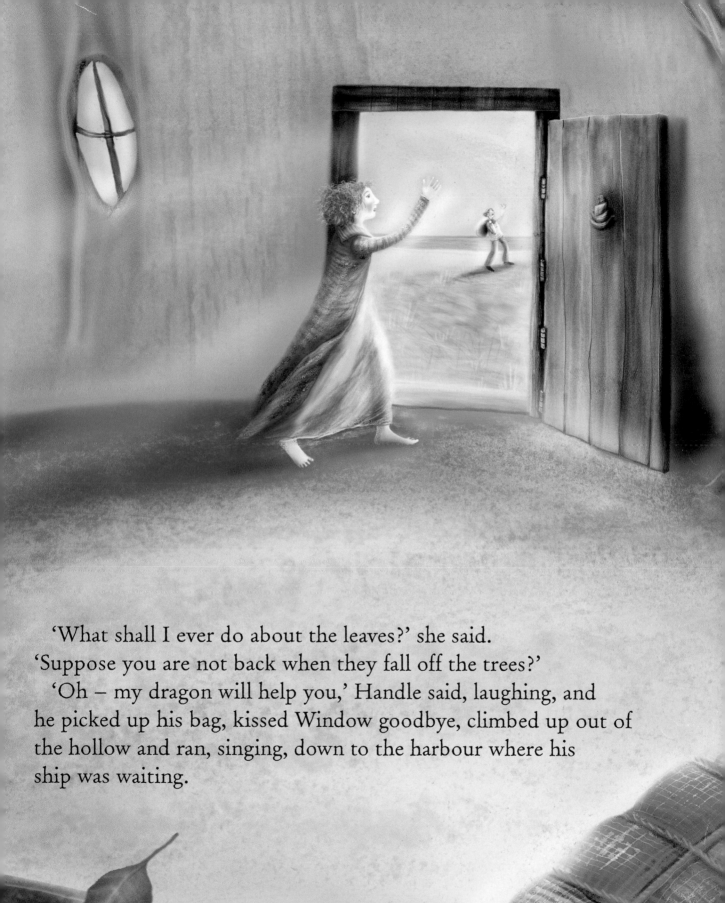

'What shall I ever do about the leaves?' she said.
'Suppose you are not back when they fall off the trees?'
   'Oh – my dragon will help you,' Handle said, laughing, and
he picked up his bag, kissed Window goodbye, climbed up out of
the hollow and ran, singing, down to the harbour where his
ship was waiting.

And he sailed away over the blue sea.

Window missed him sadly. The house was very quiet without his cheerful songs as he dug the vegetable bed or chopped the firewood. Window stopped telling stories, so no people came to hear them. The only sound was the tick of the clock as Window knitted socks or caps or sweaters. They piled up in heaps all over the house.

And the dragon? He stood on a shelf and Window never thought about him at all. He looked at her with his bright eyes and peaked forehead and hopeful mouth. He looked as if he wanted to smile, wanted to fly – but Window never turned her eyes his way. He grew dusty.

Now it was winter. The wind cried through the trees round Window's little house. Snow fell. But Window never noticed the cold. She was worrying all the time about what would happen next autumn if Handle had not come back to sweep the fallen leaves.

Those leaves have not even grown yet, thought the little dragon.

Summer followed spring. The sun was hot and apples ripened on the trees. But Window never walked outside, she sat worrying and knitting. Piles of knitted things lay all over the floor.

The little dragon on his dusty shelf grew sadder
and sadder. His eyes shone no longer.
They were too dusty. If only
I could speak, he thought.

Now the mornings began to be cold and crisp. One or two leaves fell. Then five or six. Then a great gale swept through the trees and blew all the leaves off the branches. Window's little house was buried right up to its chimney pots. Inside the house it was quite dark. The windows were covered in leaves.

Window was terrified. What shall I do? she thought. What shall I ever do? I shall die here in the cold and dark, under the leaves with nobody to help me. Then she went to bed.

As she fell asleep she thought she heard somebody crying.

In her sleep, Window began to dream. She dreamed that she found a back door to her house that she had never noticed before. The door was locked. But in her pocket she found a key. She put the key in the keyhole and it fitted. She turned the key, unlocked the door, and went outside.

At the back of the house she found a grassy patch and here
the little dragon sat crying.

'Why are you crying?' Window asked.

'My eyes are full of dust! My mouth is full of dust! My ears
are full of dust! My wings are so dusty that I can't fly.'

'I'll dust you,' said Window and she picked handfuls of grass
and gave the dragon a good rub so that he shone.

He cheered up and began to sing. Dust poured out of his
mouth. He coughed and sneezed.

'That's better!' he said. 'But my ears are still full of dust.
Tell me a story.'

So Window told him a beautiful story about a secret magic
island. But there was still some dust in his mouth and it made
him sneeze again. Window sneezed too.

The sneeze woke her out of her dream. She found that she was still in her bed, in her house, in the dark. The windows were blocked by leaves.

And not far away, somebody was crying.

'Is that you, Dragon?' asked Window.

A sneeze was the only answer. Aaaaaaa-tschooooo!

Window got out of bed. She lit a lamp. She went to the shelf where the dragon was sitting, covered in dust.

'Poor dragon!' said Window.

She took a cloth and wiped him all over. Then she rubbed and rubbed till he shone. Then she told him a story.

'That's better!' said the dragon, then, 'That's much better! It has cleared my ears, but your story makes me so, so, so hungry!'

'What would you like to eat?' asked Window.

'Open the door, and you'll see!'

Window opened the front door. As soon as she did so a
huge pile of leaves blew in all over the floor.

And the dragon ate them! He opened his mouth and sucked.
The leaves all whirled up from the floor and down his throat.
He looked up at Window and smiled a wide happy smile.
'Leaves,' he said. 'Leaves are what I like to eat.'

He went out of the door and flew round and round and
round the house, sucking and munching and crunching
until not a single leaf was left.

Then he flew down to Window, who was standing in the doorway, and said, 'Now I am going to my secret magic island. I'm tired out. I need a rest. But I will come back to help you next year when the leaves fall again.' And he flew away through the bare trees.

Window went back into the house and lit the kitchen fire.
She sat beside it, knitting. She told herself a story.
    And another story. And another.
    By and by people came to listen to her stories.
And she gave them all the things she had knitted.
    Soon, thought Window, my brother
will come home.

She looked hopeful. Almost
as hopeful as the little dragon!